Koku Baboni

Kola Onadipe

CONTENTS

ADIAS DREAM

Adia woke up one morning feeling sad.

"I am a rich woman, I have a lot of money, many farms and cattle and a lot of servants. I have everything that money can buy, but I have no children. My only daughter is dead, my husband is dead too," she said to herself.

"I am getting old," she went on. "To whom shall I give all these things when I die? I cannot have a child now. What shall I do?"

She wept and wept and there was no one to help her. She called one of her servants.

"Jilo, I am not feeling well. I am going to lie in bed all day. I don't want to see anyone."

Jilo went away. She wondered why "Mami" was so unhappy

Adia lay in bed. She wrapped herself up, from head to toe, with her big cloth. Again she wept. Then she fell asleep and did not wake up for a long time.Suddenly she jumped up and was awake. She had dreamt a dream.

In her dream, a woman came to her. She was tall and thin. Her skin was light brown. She was dressed in white from her neck to her toes. The dress was as white as paper. It covered every part of her body, even her fingers. The hair on her head was almost white. It was soft and long. The woman's face was soft. It was like the face of a fine young girl.

She came and stood in front of Adia. There seemed to be more light in the room, yet there was no lamp burning. She smiled at Adia and put her finger on her mouth to tell Adia not to shout.

This woman was the most pleasing person Adia had seen in her life. She looked kind and good. Adia spoke softly."Who are you? Are you a Queen or something? Are you an angel? You look happy and sweet. I am a sad woman. I wish I could be as happy as you. Come, live with me. I shall give you a good room. I shall dress the room and bed in white. Hold my hand and let us be friends. I shall call you the 'Lady-in-white' and you will call me Adia.

"The visitor answered. "You have a kind heart, Adia. We are friends already but don't let us hold hands yet. Stay where you are and don't try to get up. "I know you are sad. I know you are rich. Yet you are not happy. You are sad because you do not have a son to whom you can leave your riches. I want to help you because you have been helping others and because you love children.

"Get up very early tomorrow morning as soon as the cock crows. Take with you a small clean basket. Take some soap and a cloth. Go by yourself. Do not take a servant with you. Don't be afraid.

"Go towards Idiala, the big village by the great river. You should get there before the wine tappers go out. You will meet no one on the way. Take the last path on your left before you reach the village. Follow it until you come to the place where a small stream joins the great river.

Stand there and listen. From then on you will be a happy woman." The Lady-in-white stopped speaking. "Now I leave you. I may come again. Good-bye!"

Adia jumped up to follow the woman and she woke up. "So I have been dreaming."

She was sorry it was a dream and she said, "But I have never dreamt like this before. I shall do what I was told in my dream. The Lady-in-white asked me to go there and listen. Listen to what? This is strange.I shall tell no one but I shall do what she told me to do."

ADIA FINDS A BABY

That night the visitor did not come. Adia wanted her to come and finish the story. Adia did not sleep much. Perhaps that was why the visitor did not come.When the first cock crowed. Adia opened the door softly and went out.She took with her a small basket, some soap and a clean piece of cloth.

It was very dark. There was no moonlight. Adia could not see her way easily. She therefore went slowly along the bush path. The morning dew had made the long grass wet. She pulled up her wrapper but her legs were wet and cold.

She went on. She was alone. A small animal ran across the path in front of her. It moved the bush as it ran along. Adia was at first afraid. She stopped and looked around her. It was too dark to see any. thing well. An owl cried nearby and she saw his big bright eyes. The eyes shone like fire. Adia was not afraid because she knew it was only an owl.

Soon she started to see more clearly. She was getting tired because she had been walking for a long time. Still she met no one. She was near the village. She could hear the frogs and water insects. She knew now that she was very close to a stream.

She came to the path which the "Lady-in-white" told her to follow. She turned and followed the path. She soon came to the spot where the small stream joined the great river.

She stood there and listened. Nothing happened. She listened again for some time. She heard nothing. She sat down and listened for a long time. She felt like sleeping and closed her eyes.

The "Lady-in-white" stood in front of Adia. "Don't sleep, Adia; listen now," she said. Adia woke up quickly and the lady was gone. She listened and from somewhere near she heard,

"Pihen! Pihen!! Pihen!!!" "That sounds like a baby crying," Adia thought.

She listened again. She was now sure it was a baby crying. She moved towards the place where the crying came from.

"That sounds like a baby crying," Adia thought.

She listened again. She was now sure it was a baby crying. She moved towards the place where the crying came from.

Right there in front of her was a calabash. It was caught in the bush at the edge of the small stream. The cry came from inside this calabash. The calabash had been rubbed on the outside with palm oil.

Adia ran forward and there lying on a rag inside the calabash was a baby boy. He wore nothing but was kicking hard. He rubbed his face with his hands and cried out louder. Adia looked with surprise on this baby and she was moved with pity. Tears ran down her cheeks.

It was a pretty baby boy. There were some red spots on his body where insects had bitten it. There was palm oil all over the baby. Some cooked yam pieces soaked in palm oil were in the calabash too.

Adia picked up the baby...

"What am I to do with it now? Whose child is it?" She wondered. "It is very dirty." She remembered the soap and cloth she had brought and said, "Truly this is what the 'Lady-in-white' meant."

She sat down and washed the baby clean with the soap and cloth. She wrapped up the baby and put it in the basket.

She got some clean water and fed the baby with it. The baby stopped crying. Adia touched his face and smiled at the baby. She held him up and kissed him on the lips.

"What a beautiful baby you are! Now I know God has sent you to me. I will take you home and you will be my son," Adia said.

She put the baby back in the small basket. She picked up the basket and carried it under her arm.As she went she often looked and smiled at the baby.The baby did not cry any more. It fell asleep and did not wake for a long time

. Adia was now very near home.

"What shall I say to the people? I don't even know how the baby came to be there in the bush," she thought. She went straight to the chief's house and told the story of the baby boy. She begged the chief to let her keep the boy.

When the chief heard the story he laughed and said, "Have no fear, Adia, the gods have given you a son. You shall keep him and bring him up and no one will worry you

"The people of Idiala have a strange custom. We do not have it here in this town. They believe that twin children are evil. They believe that twin children bring evil to the village and to their family.

Sometimes twin children and their mothers are sent out of the village and are left to be killed by wild animals and, or to die of hunger in the bush. At other times only the twin children are killed. Sometimes when their father is an important man the twin children are not killed straight away. They are put in a calabash. Some pieces of boiled yam soaked in palm oil are put in the calabash. The calabash is rubbed on the outside with palm oil. The two calabashes are then placed in a stream. Often the babies kick and the calabashes turn over and the babies drown."

The chief went on, "This time one of the calabashes must have been caught in the grass at the edge of the river. If you had not picked it up, this baby too would have died.

"Go in peace and keep your baby. I shall tell the townspeople."

Adia was happy because she had found a son. But she was not happy because the other twin baby was either dead already or was about to die.

"Should I go and look for the other baby?" she asked herself. "I cannot leave this one, yet I cannot take him with me. But the other baby is sure to be dead by now," she said to herself.

Adia went home. She called her servants together and gave them the news.

"I have today found a son to whom I shall give all my money. I am now a happy woman. It will be your duty to take care of him in every way you can.

"Jilo, you will bring this baby up as the son of a chief. I shall name him Koku Baboni. It is Koku because he would not die. It is Baboni because God answered my prayer."

KOKU GROWS UP

For many days and many weeks after the arrival of Koku Baboni in Adia's house there was feasting.People came in great numbers from the town, men, women, boys and girls. They came to see the boy who wouldn't die. They came to greet the kind Adia. They came to show that they loved Adia who loved children.They all loved Koku.

Many of them brought gifts for the little baby:Many of them went back with bigger gifts from Adia. Adia was happy and she spent a lot of money making herself and others happy

Many of the visitors came in groups, clapping their hands, singing and dancing. Adia joined them. They laughed, ate, drank and were happy.

Every Friday, Adia fed the little children of the town. They too ate, sang and clapped their hands.But all these visitors could only look at Koku. They were not allowed to touch him. Only Jilo and one other maid-servant touched him.

Adia took great care of Koku. She loved the baby. She would watch him sleep. She would put her ear near his nose to make sure he was breathing.

She fed Koku very well. Soon he would smile and throw his hands and legs up while lying on his back whenever Adia came in. This made Adia happy. "Koku now knows me," she said.

Soon Koku began to call "Ma" and to stand up. He grew up very healthy and strong.

In the morning and in the evening Adia put Koku on her knees and told him a lot of things. But Koku was too young to understand.

Koku grew up in the town. He was loved by everyone. He was loved because Adia, his mother, was kind and good. He was loved because he was a handsome lad and because he was good. He was always happy and smiling. He was good to everybody. He played with other children. They followed him home and he followed them home. He ate with them in their homes, no matter how poor the food. They ate with him too in his home. Adia did not stop him from mixing with other children. This made the parents of the children love Koku more.

Whenever any of Koku's friends was ill, Adia would walk there holding Koku, by the hand.

Koku was growing fast. He was now a much bigger boy than other boys of his age. He was much stronger too. When they wrestled Koku was always the winner.

When they ran Koku always came first. Even older boys could not beat him. The boys did not dislike him for this. Koku became their leader.

Koku was soon known all over the town because he was strong, good and kind.

So the people were not surprised Koku was Adia's child.

Adia loved Koku more and more every day. She was very pleased with him. She loved to see him run, swim and wrestle, beating the other boys.

Every time Koku came back home Adia would look at him very closely. She would feel every part of his body to make sure he was not hiding any cut as boys will do. She had many medicines to give Koku should he ever be ill. But then something happened.

KOKU IS ILL

After breakfast one day Koku went out with other boys. They did not come back home in time for the midday meal. Adia was worried. She called two of her servants.

"Go out and look for Koku. He has not come home for his lunch. He does not often miss his meals. Something must have happened to him. Go quickly and don't come back until you find him."

Adia was very worried. She could not sit in one place for long. She could not stand in one place for long either. She was sitting down and getting up all the time. She looked out many times but did not see Koku.

She sent her other servants to go to the houses of Koku's friends. They came back to say that the friends were also away from home.

While this was going on, Koku was lying on his back under the shade of a tree. He was weak and breathing very slowly. His friends were throwing water from the stream on him because he had fainted. They had taken off his clothes. But the boys were young and did not know what to do

At last they decided that two out of them will go to the town to say that Koku was dying. These two boys had not gone far when they met the two servants whom Adia had sent to look for Koku. The two boys told the story

"We were chasing birds and rats in the bush for a long time. The sun was shining bright and we felt very hot. We were hungry and so we picked some pawpaw fruits and ate. They were not ripe but we ate them all the same," said one boy.

Instead of returning home we went farther and farther into the bush. Then all of a sudden, Koku shouted, 'My bead, my back? The next minute he was lying on the ground. He couldn't move his arms or legs. His eyes were just open. They did not move. He wouldn't speak," the other boy added.

We pulled off his clothes and poured water on him. We were near a stream. But Koku would not move. Then we came running home to tell his mother." The servants ran with the two boys back to the place where Koku was lying. They saw Koku and were afraid.

"What would Mami do if this boy died?" one asked. "Don't talk about death. Koku is not going to die. How can such a good boy die?" the other answered. He was angry.

Quickly they put Koku's clothes on him and one of them carried him on his back. Koku's hands were hanging down by his sides. He looked as if he was already dead.

Adia jumped up and threw herself down in tears. She shouted for help. She wept aloud and people, men, women and children ran to her.They all saw Koku and all felt sad. They pitied

Koku. They also felt sorry for Adia.

Some women were holding Adia in order to stop her from hurting herself. The men had laid Koku down on a bed.

They were now running to bring whatever medicine they had. They worked on him for some time and then someone shouted.

"He is moving his hands." Soon Koku opened his eyes. He was sick. Then he sneezed. At last he spoke."Where am I? Where is Mami? My head is hurting. so is my back."

Adia came running to Koku. They held each other. Tears came down from Adia's eyes.

Koku was carried to his bed in his room. He did not faint again but he was very ill. On the third day the illness became worse. Medicine men were coming in and going out. Adia was very worried.

Adia could not sleep at first, but, when she slept, she dreamt. In her dream, she saw that there was a bright light in her room. In front of her stood the "Lady-in-white' again.

She smiled at Adia but Adia did not smile. Her son was dying.

"Do not weep, Adia," said the Lady-in-white.

"Koku will not die". The gods who gave him to you will not take him away now. He will become great and will live long after you."

"Make him well quickly then, please, Lady-in-white," cried Adia. "I hate to see him so ill like this. He can't eat. He can't move. Will he ever be strong again?"

"Don't fear, Koku will be even stronger. Get up now. Put some water in a clean pot and leave it out-side.

Don't cover it. Let the dew fall on it."Stop the medicine men from giving him more medicine. They do not know what they are doing. They can't help him. They will only make him worse.

Tomorrow at noon, bathe Koku with the water in the pot and let him sleep after that."

Adia woke up. The Lady-in-white had gone.side. Don't cover it. Let the dew fall on it.

"Stop the medicine men from giving him more medicine. They do not know what they are doing.

They can't help him. They will only make him worse.

Tomorrow at noon, bathe Koku with the water in the pot and let him sleep after that."

Adia woke up. The Lady-in-white had gone.

"So I have been dreaming again," Adia said, still feeling sad. She got up and went to Koku's room. He was still very ill. The medicine men stood round watching him. Koku was growing weaker and weaker.

The medicine men seemed to be waiting for him to die. Adia herself washed the pot and put in clean water and left it in the dew. She did not sleep again that night. On the following day, just before noon, Adia called the medicine men and spoke to them.

"I thank you all very much for your love and for everything you have done. It does not seem that my son is going to get well this way. I have killed many rams, goats and fowls. I have bought many yards of white clothes. I will gladly buy many more if I am sure they can make my son well. As you know, you cannot buy a son in the market

"Allow me to try something different. I am going to give Koku some of this water to drink. I am going to bathe him with what remains."

"Please do not try it," the medicine men said together. "It will surely kill him. You cannot cure this illness with cold water. But you can see that your son is getting well."

"I cannot see that he is any better than he was

He is even weaker. I am going to bathe him. If he dies then I know that the one who gave him to me has taken him away."

The medicine men left the room one by one. Adia spoke to the last of them

"Help me bring the boy out into the yard and help me hold him while I bathe him.

The medicine man agreed although he was afraid the boy might die in his hands. But Koku did not die while having his bath. He was taken back to his room.

The room had been swept clean and all the pots, shells and feathers, which the medicine men used, were taken away,

Koku was laid on the bed. He was soon fast asleep. Adia sat by him. Her eyes did not leave Koku's face. She watched every move of his face and every move of his body.

It was almost night when Koku woke up. He shouted, "Don't go, don't go," and then opened his eyes.

"Whom are you talking to, Koku?" asked Adia. "I thought it was you, Mami. A woman sat by me. She was dressed in white. She gave me something very sweet to drink. She rubbed every part of my body with oil and it was cool. Then she said that she was going and that I should go out to visit my friends in the morning."

Adia knew it was the Lady-in-white. She had told Adia that Koku would be well.

When it was morning, Koku was able to get up and walk. Everybody was surprised. The medicine men were more surprised. They had thought that Koku would die after the bath.

Adia was happy once again. She killed all sorts of animals and fowls and feasted those who came to greet her and Koku. Once again Koku and his friends could be together and play together as before.

KOKU MAKES A FRIEND

Koku was now about twelve years old. But he was very big for his age. One day he and two other friends were returning home from the bush. They came to a place where a woman was gathering firewood. She was not very old but she looked poor. Her dress was torn here and there. Koku watched this woman and felt sorry for her.

He had not seen her before. His two other friends knew her very well. Koku again stopped to watch this woman. His friends called."Koku, come let us go home, leave the woman alone."

Koku followed them but he was thinking of the woman. He wanted to talk to her and help her. When they reached the town, Koku spoke to his friends.

"Go home, I am going out soon with Mami. I'll be seeing you tonight."

As soon as his friends had gone home, Koku ran back the way they had come. He was going to see the woman. He ran further. He saw her.

She had tied up the firewood and was trying to lift it onto her head.

She bent down to pick up the firewood and she fell back into the bush. She started to try again.

"Stop it." Koku shouted to her, "I will help you."He picked up the firewood easily and placed it on his head.

"Thank you, my son, may God bless you," answered the woman.

"You should not be doing this by yourself. Why don't you ask your children to fetch the firewood for you?" asked Koku.

The old woman did not answer. She simply sighed, and shook her head. Tears came into her eyes. She quickly wiped them away. She did not want Koku to see that she was weeping. But he had seen it.

"Come along. I shall carry it home for you. This is too heavy for you."

Koku was surprised. He wondered why the woman wept. "Perhaps she has no child," he thought.

They did not speak for the rest of the way. They soon reached her house. It was not a poor house, It was not as poor as Koku expected. Inside, the house was clean.

"Isn't there anyone in the house?" Koku asked

"I live alone here," she answered.

"Have you no children?"

"I have one, a daughter, but she is not here now."

"Is she gone to her husband then?" asked Koku.

"My daughter is too young to marry," she answered. "She is only eleven. She has gone..." The woman could not finish the sentence. She began to weep and dry the tears with the end of her wrapper which she held up.

Koku did not understand. He knew however, that this woman was not happy. He did not like to see people sad.

"But why are you crying?" he asked the woman.

"Is there anything wrong with your daughter? No. I will not ask you again. You will tell me all about it some other time. Promise."

"I promise," answered the woman.understand. "Is there anything I can do for you before I go?

Shall I fill your pot with water? Shall I cut wood for you?" Koku asked.

"You are a kind young man. Who are you and who is your mother? The boys around here are not usually so kind."

"I shan't tell you my name today. I'll come here again tomorrow. Then you will tell me about your daughter and I will tell you about myself," answered Koku.

"If you don't tell me your name before you go, I am going to give you a name," the woman said smiling. "The name is 'Handsome'."

"I don't mind what you call me but I shan't tell you my name today," answered Koku laughing.

Koku did not tell his name and the name of his mother because he thought that the woman would know all about him if he did.

The next day, Koku would not go out with his friends. But soon after his friends had gone, Koku went out. He went straight to the woman's house.

"I hope I have not come too early," he said as soon as he entered the house.

"Handsome, you are not too early. I have been looking out for you. I am glad to have you here," she answered.

"Thank you. How are you feeling today?" asked Koku.

"I am feeling fine, thank you too. How is your mother?" she answered.

"She is well, thank you."

"By the way, are you Adia's son? Are you Koku?" she asked.

"How do you know? Have you been asking about me since I left you yesterday?" asked Koku laughing

"I have asked no one about you. But I have heard a lot about you. I have been told that you are kind, handsome and good. When you left yesterday, I sat down and started to think. You do not find many boys like you around here," she answered.

"Since you already know, I am Koku, son of Adia," said Koku. "I am not surprised, because Adia is a good woman. She is a lucky woman to be so rich, to have such a kind heart and, on top of it all, to have a son like you.

Every woman would love to have a son like you, Handsome. I am happy for you that you have such a fine mother," answered the woman.

"But you have not been coming to visit my mother.

Don't you like her?" asked Koku.

"I came to see you when you came to her, but that was a long time ago," she answered. "I have not been coming because I have a lot of difficulties of my own.

I am not a happy woman. There is no reason why I should not like your mother. She has been kind to me many times. She knows me very well. We have both lived in the same town all.our lives.

"I see you are not happy; but why? Is it because of your daughter? Won't you tell me about yourself and about your daughter?" he asked.

"It is a long story, I don't like thinking about it or telling people about it. It makes me sad. But I shall tell you about it," answered the woman. "Let me give you some bean balls which I have made for you.

They may not be as good as the ones your mother's servants make for you. I hope you will eat them all the same. I used to make them for my daughter."

"I am not hungry but I will eat them. I do not care whether or not they are good," Koku answered. "My mother won't mind."

SALA'S STORY

While Koku ate the bean balls, the woman told him her story. "My name is Sala. I have always lived in this town. So too had my husband. He was born of rich parents and he was their only son. My parents were not as rich as his parents but they were not very poor.

"When my husband, Ladi, married me, everyone was happy about it. We loved each other very much.

Ladi's parents gave him every help. So, too, did my parents help me. We had nothing to worry about.

"Ladi's parents helped him to build this house soon after our marriage. We moved in and we were happy.

"We had six children but only Kemi, my daughter, the last born, lived. All the others died very young.

Still we were happy together. My husband did not marry another wife. Before his parents died, they advised him to marry another wife. But Ladi would not do so.

"Then about five years ago, Ladi became ill. It was a very bad illness. I was worried. His parents and my parents were already dead. I was left alone to look after him. Kemi was only six years old then.

"I tried all I could to care for him. I called in medicine men from far and near. They asked for a lot of money, goats, fowls, white cloth and so on. They got them. But Ladi did not get better.

"Ladi called me one day and said, 'Don't give more money and things to medicine men. Save up what is left so that when I am gone you will have enough to live upon and to bring up Kemi.'

"I did not listen. I could not see my husband die like that. So I went on spending money. When there was no more to be spent, I sold our farms and almost all that we had."*I woke up one morning and Ladi was dead. I wept and wept. Kemi was too young to understand. She sat on my knees all the time I was weeping. I held her closely to me. She was all that I had left, I didn't have enough money to pay for the funeral.

I had to borrow. I needed about ten pounds but I had nothing. There was nobody to lend me money. Then one day a man from Idiala came to me. He said that he learnt I needed money badly. He would lend me ten pounds, but my daughter would have to work for him until I could pay him back. My daughter would have to leave home and go to him at Idiala. When I got the money, he would give me my daughter back.

"At first I did not know what to do. I did not want my only daughter to go away. I thought I could not live without her. Yet I knew that I must get money for the funeral. There was no one else to give it to me. The funeral must be done immediately.

"I therefore told Kemi what was to happen. She agreed to go and work for this man. So I took the money.

"Three days after the funeral, Kemi left for Idiala.

We both wept and wept. I promised Kemi that she would soon come back to me. I was going to get money somewhere to pay the man back.

"I have not seen Kemi since. I have not heard anything of her since. The man, Akila, has never called here. I am too ashamed to go to Idiala to see Kemi.""Everybody who knew the story was sorry for me but no one gave me money. So Kemi, my dear girl, Kemi, my little girl, is working hard because of me.

I have not been able to get the money. My health has not been good. I am finding it difficult to feed myself.

See me in rags, I cannot buy any clothes. I don't even care about that. I am thinking of Kemi every day.She may never come back to me. Where shall I get the money? Maybe I shall die without seeing her. She must be very sad there. Perhaps they beat her there.

Perhaps they do not feed her well. Kemi, my gentle daughter, is now a slave." As she spoke she wept again. Koku tried to comfort her but she would not stop crying. But why didn't you tell my mother? She could help you, She has money," said Koku,

"No! No! your mother will not lend money, She likes to give. She has many other people to help," the woman answered,

"But she will gladly help you. Let me speak to her. You must bring Kemi back, She must be unhappy there. It is not right," said Koku.

"I don't want you to tell your mother, Promise me you will not tell her, Will you promise?" she asked.

"I promise," answered Koku, "Don't tell me more about Kemi, It makes me too sad, Don't let us talk about her again, But don't weep; Kemi will surely come back," said Koku,

Koku left the woman's house feeling very unhappy.

He knew that the woman was unhappy and would not be happy until her daughter came back home, Koku knew too that Kemi could not be happy where she was. How could she be happy? She had not seen her mother for a long time and she was living with strangers,

Koku went home, He could not eat well that afternoon,

"Koku has not eaten well this afternoon, Mami; he does not speak to anyone, He has been lying on his bed. Maybe he is ill," Jilo told Adia, Adia went to Koku's room,

"What is wrong, Baboni? Are you sick?" she asked,

"I am not sick, Mami, I just want to be left alone for some time. Don't worry about me," he answered. Adia touched his face to see if he had a fever. But his face was not hot.

"Tell me, Babont, have you hurt yourself?"

"No, Mami." said Koku

"Good," said Adia, "take care of yourself." Then she left him.

Koku spent most of his time for the next three days with Kemi's mother. He learnt more about Akila, where he lived, and how to get to Idiala.

On the night of the third day, Koku went to his mother and said, "Please give me ten pounds and don't ask yet what I want to do with it. I shall tell you later."

The mother thought for a minute and then answered, "I shall give you ten pounds. You want it for a good reason. You have never asked for money. I know you need this and I will give it to you. But you must tell me everything later."

Koku promised to tell her. He got the money that night and was very happy. Everybody noticed that Koku was happy. The mother saw this and smiled. She knew that the ten pounds had made him happy.

KOKU GOES TO IDIALA

The next morning, immediately after breakfast, Koku went out. He told no one where he was going or what he was going to do.

He took with him the ten pounds which his mother had given him. He also took with him some other money of his own.

He left the town and went along the path that led to Idiala. He had learnt from Sala how to get to Idiala. He thought he could get to Idiala and back before evening.

Koku had not visited Idiala before. He did not know that he was born there and that his real parents lived there. He had always thought that he was Adia's son.Koku went out. He told no one where he was going or what he was going to do.

He took with him the ten pounds which his mother had given him. He also took with him some other money of his own. As he went along, he had no fear of anything. He was happy even though he was alone. He was going to bring Kemi back to her mother. It would be a big surprise to her and they were going to be happy. The woman would not have to fetch firewood and water by herself. Kemi would do all that for her.

He had never seen Kemi. All he knew was that she was a girl. Perhaps she was a fat girl, perhaps she was a thin girl. Whatever she was, he was going to love her like a sister. He had always wanted a sister. Perhaps his mother, Adia, would allow Kemi to live with him and be his sister.

These thoughts made him happy. Sometimes he was so happy that he ran instead of walking. As he went along the bush path he took a stick and beat the bush.

At other times he sang happily.

Before long, he reached Idiala. He walked faster.

He wanted to see Kemi soon and take her home.

"I am not afraid; why should I be afraid? I am not doing anything wrong, why should anyone want to hurt me?"

It was easy to find Akila's house. He was well known for he was a rich man. Koku went straight to the big compound which was fenced round with bamboo and palm leaves.

He opened the gate and saw no one. He shouted.

"Who is here?"

Then some boys looked out from other doors nearby.

One boy came out. He was older and bigger than Koku.

"Why are you making such a noise? Where do you think you are, you silly boy?" he asked Koku.

"That is not the way to speak to visitors. I shall tell your master, "Koku answered.

"You tell my master what? Before you tell my master i shall teach you how to speak to your elders, said the boy.

He came near to Koku, pulled his nose and hit him on the face. Two other boys who had come out started to laugh.

"Give him more," said one of them.

The first boy drew near to give Koku another hit.

Koku caught his hand, pulled him suddenly towards himself and gave him a kick in the stomach with his knee.

The boy shouted, "He is killing me!" and fell down weeping and shouting with pain.

The other two boys came near. They held their fists in front of them. Koku moved as if he was going to run away. He turned away, and took a few steps. One of the boys came after him. Koku turned around suddenly. He shot out his fist. It hit the boy in the mouth and he fell down. He was bleeding at the mouth and shouting.

The other boy seeing this ran away shouting, "Here is a mad boy!"

The older people came out and there was much noise in the compound. One man came forward and said, "Who is the boy and where is he from?" Koku would not answer the question.

"I want to see Akila," was all he said.

"You cannot see him until we know who you are and what your business is," the man said.

"That you will not know," answered Koku.

"Give him a beating and push him out," shouted someone

"Yes! yes!!" said the others.

Someone was coming forward to beat Koku, when a woman, who had been standing in front of the big house, shouted, "Bring the boy here before you do anything, and keep quiet all of you."

There was silence while someone led Koku by the hand to the woman.

When Koku came near and the woman saw his face, she just stood there. She did not say anything. She kept on looking at the boy's face.

Koku too looked at the woman's face. He seemed to have seen her before. The people who stood around looked from the boy's face to the woman's face. They saw that the faces were alike. They did not understand. Nobody understood.

Then the woman spoke again."Boy, I understand you want to see Akila. You shall see him immediately. Those of you standing round, get back to your rooms. Don't you worry this boy any more."

KOKU MEETS KEMI

This woman, Abi by name, held Koku's hand. As she did so she felt she loved this boy as a son.

"Come and see Akila, my husband," she said. "But tell me your name."

"My name is Koku," he answered. "I come from Ihama. But you are a kind woman. You are like my mother."

"And you are a nice boy, handsome and strong. I wish you were my son," she said. "Will your mother allow you to come and see me often?"

"I am the only son of my mother. She doesn't want me to leave her even for a day," he answered.

Now they had come to where Akila was sitting. He was smoking a long pipe, and chewing kolanut.

He had a bottle of palm wine on the ground near him.

A boy was sitting on the ground beside him. The boy held a calabash cup of palm wine in his hand. He was waiting for Akila to take it from his hand.

"It is you again so soon, Abi. Has that girl, Kemi, done anything wrong again? She is always weeping.

She wants to go home to her mother but I can't lose my twelve pounds," he said.

Koku heard this. He was happy to know that Kemi still loved her mother but he was afraid. He had brought only ten pounds and this man had said he wanted twelve pounds.

"It is not Kemi at all. Poor girl! I wish you would let that girl go home. She says her mother is old. But here is a boy, Koku by name, who wants to see you. He says he is from Ihama,

"Come forward, lad, let's hear you," he said.

Koku moved forward and started to speak. He saw the man's face and stopped. The man was looking at Koku's face and also at Abi's face. Koku wondered why everybody was doing this. Then the man spoke.

"Abi, why? This lad looks very much like you.

One would think you were his mother," he said.

"I am surprised too, I have seen it. And somehow I love the boy," she answered.

"Now, Koku, let us hear you," Akila said.

Koku went down on his knees and spoke.

"I have been sent here by Kemi's mother from Thama to pay you ten pounds and bring Kemi back. The mother is too old to walk here herself." "But she should pay twelve pounds. She borrowed ten pounds five years ago," Akila answered.

"I didn't know that. She did not know either," Koku explained

"She should know. She ought to know. Go back to her and bring the two pounds. Tell her Kemi has not been useful. She is often ill," he said.

"Please, I beg you, let me pay you this ten pounds and I will bring you the two pounds. Let me take Kemi back to her mother," Koku begged.

"Go away, come back in the evening. I'll think about it and will let you know what I decide," Akila said. "I have nowhere to go. I know no one here. Let me stay in your compound till the evening," answered Koku.

"Come with me," said Abi. "I will take care of you till the evening."

Abi and Koku left Akila. Koku had a wash and felt fine. He had a nice meal and then slept.

When Koku awoke from his sleep, he found Abi and a boy of about ten sitting on the same mat watching him.

"How do you feel now, Koku?" asked Abi.

"Fine, thank you," he replied.

"Koku, this is my son Sanu. He is ten. One would think he was your brother. You look very much alike.

"Sanu is the only son I have. I had two children before him. They were not allowed to live. I was not killed because my husband is a big man.

"From your look and the clothes you wear, you must have rich parents, Koku," she said.

"Yes, my mother is rich, but my father is dead.

I like Sanu. Will you allow him to visit me sometimes?" Koku asked.

"If his father will allow it," she answered. In the evening, Abi took Koku back to Akila.

"Koku, I have heard more about you since you left this place in the morning. I like you. I like you because you are strong and handsome and you know what you want.

"My wife here, Abi, came back to me to speak for you. It seems everyone likes you," Akila said. "Bring the ten pounds."

"Abi, call Kemi for me. You Koku, can take her away. I will not even ask for the two pounds," he added.

Kemi came in. Koku looked at her. She was very tall for her age. She was thin and looked very unhappy. As she came in she looked very frightened.

She moved in slowly, looking downward.

"I haven't done anything wrong, I was just sitting," she said.

"Stop that!" Akila shouted. "No one is asking you a question."

When Koku saw the girl, he felt very sorry for her. Kemi was unhappy. She looked as if she had not eaten for some time. Yet she was a pretty girl. Koku wanted to run to the girl and take her hand and say many kind things to her. But he waited to hear what Akila would say or do. If Akila beat that girl, he, Koku, would fight him.

But Akila did not beat Kemi, Abi moved near the girl like a mother. She wiped her face with the edge of her cloth.

"Don't cry again; I have always told you that. You will soon be a happy girl," Abi said.

"Am I going home to my mother then?" Kemi asked.

"Yes, you are going home to your mother. This young man here will take you home. He has been sent by your mother to bring you," Akila said.

Kemi could not believe it at first. She looked at Koku. She did not know him.

"Is it a joke?" she thought.

Koku smiled at her and put out his arms to her.

Kemi ran into his open arms, threw her arms round his neck and buried her face on his chest. She wept and shook with the weeping. She wept like this for some time. Then Abi, who was almost weeping too, went to pull Kemi off. Kemi still held Koku's hand and would not let go.

"It is now too late for you to go back to Ihama.

You will stay the night here and then go away first thing tomorrow morning, Koku," said Akila.

"I know it is late. But, if I do not go, my mother will not sleep tonight. She does not know where ! am," Koku answered."You will tell her tomorrow when you get home.

You and Kemi will come with me for the night. In the morning I will lead you part of the way," said Abi.

KEMI COMES HOME

At Ihama, it was time for lunch, and Koku had not come home. Adia and her servants were worried. The servants went round Koku's friends but none of them had seen Koku that day.

Adia knew that Koku had gone somewhere to spend the ten pounds. But where?

One of Koku's friends said, "You better look for him at Sala's house. He has been spending much of his time with her." Adia herself went there and asked.

"I have not seen Koku today. He used to come and help me here. He is such a nice young man," Sala said. "He was here yesterday."

Then Sala was worried."When did he leave home?" she asked Adia.

"He left home this morning after breakfast. When he came home last night he was unhappy. He asked me for ten pounds and I gave it to him.

He did not tell me what he wanted it for," Adia said."Ten pounds! ten pounds!! ten pounds!!!" Sala repeated many times. "Then I know," she said.

Sala told Adia all that she had told Koku about her daughter, Kemi, and how she could not find ten pounds to bring her back from Idiala.

"I am sure Koku has gone to Idiala to Akila." When Adia heard that, she was afraid.

"Someone might tell Koku about his birth and he will no longer love me as his mother," she thought.She quickly called some of her man-servants and Jilo. They left the town and took the road that led to Idiala. It was evening already.

They walked very fast, but it was getting dark when they reached Idiala. They went straight to Akila's house. Adia went in to see him. She told him why she had come.

"I am pleased to know you. You have a fine boy, handsome, brave and strong. He is with my wife and Kemi.

"I stopped them from going back because it would be dangerous for two little children to travel at night," he said."Thank you. I must go and see Koku. Then we go back tonight," she answered.

Koku and Kemi were eating their dinner when Adia knocked.Good evening, she said. Koku jumped up and ran to the door. He held his mother's hands and begged her, "Mami, don't be angry with me. I did not know I was going to be so long, I wanted to help this girl, Kemi. I could not tell you because you might have stopped me. You might have thought that I was too young to come alone."

"It is all right now, son. But you must always tell me things like this. I am pleased with you because you are kind," she answered.

She turned to Abi to say something but she stopped. She looked at Abi's face and at Sanu's face.They both looked very much like Koku. She was afraid. In her mind she thought,

"Can this woman be the real mother of Koku? Koku was born in this village of important parents."

She quickly started to speak again to Abi. "I thank you for taking care of my — my — son."She couldn't say "my son" easily now. "We shan't stay any longer. We'll take Kemi with us. Thank you again."

"It has been a joy for me to look after your son. I don't know why but I feel as if he is my son.Perhaps you will allow him to come and see us often.

Sanu, my son, and I would like to come and see him too," Abi answered."I will let you know about that," Adia said and walked out.

Abi and Sanu went with them till they left the village. As they went back Adia was feeling sad. She wondered why Koku looked very much like that woman and her son. Adia thought that she would find out later if Abi had ever had twin children. Then she would know. "Koku must not know his own story." she thought.

Kemi's mother was very happy to see her daughter. She was happy to see Koku too. She did not know what to do to thank Koku.

That night Adia lay awake for a long time. She was thinking of Koku and the woman at Idiala. If she was Koku's real mother what would she do if she knew? What would Koku do?

At last Adia slept. She dreamt. The Lady-in-white came.

"Have no fear, Adia, about Koku. It is true that the woman you saw at Idiala is his real mother. But I gave Koku to you. Neither Koku nor that woman will know this story while you are still living. Even after your death, Koku will still think of you as his mother."When Adia woke up she was happy.

This Lady-in-white is always helping me. Who is she? I am going to ask her next time she comes," she said.

ADIA DIES

Kemi soon settled down with her mother. She helped her mother. She no longer wept. She was happy even though they were poor. Koku was always in the house to play with Kemi and to help both Kemi and her mother. He was like a brother to Kemi.

But Kemi would not go to Koku's house to play.She knew Koku's mother was rich and kind. Adia would have liked to give Kemi money. But Kemi did not want anything her own mother could not give her.

Even when Koku brought her things she would not take them.

She liked Koku very much. They would sit together and tell stories. One thing that always made Koku happy was that he liked to eat what Kemi ate.

For some years this was how they lived.Then there was a change. Koku still went to see Kemi, but Kemi did not want to see him so often. She still liked him, but she knew she was grown up now and she was too poor to buy new dresses. The only dress she had was ragged. She was always ashamed to see Koku. He was always neat and clean.

Koku also saw that Kemi was now a grown up, beautiful girl of seventeen. He was eighteen. He knew that Kemi was always ashamed to see him. He knew the reason for this. He wanted to help her but he knew Kemi would not take anything from him. He became unhappy.

"I see you are unhappy these days, Baboni," said Adia one day. "May I know why?"

"Kemi does not want to see me any more. She is ashamed because she has no clothes," he answered.

"Why don't you give her some money?" asked Adia. "She won't take it. She is ashamed of having to take money from a friend," Koku answered.

Adia knew that Koku loved Kemi, but that he was afraid to tell Kemi this.

"Why don't you marry her then, Koku? You are old enough," asked Adia.

"Do you really mean I can do that, Mami? I have been afraid to ask you. You might think I am too young or that she is too young or that she is too poor," Koku answered.

"Go now and tell her, my son," said Adia.

Koku was soon at Kemi's place.

"Kemi, I have told my mother I am going to marry you and she said 'Yes'."

"And I say 'No'. People will think because you paid the ten pounds, my mother has given me to you. They will think we want your money because we are poor, answered Kemi. When Koku told his mother the answer Kemi gave him, she laughed

"Leave it to me, my son." Adia got busy and before long Kemi had fine dresses and was often walking hand in hand with Koku.

Soon Koku and Kemi were married. Many people came to the wedding. Abi and Sanu were there. Even Akila and his friends from Idiala were there. There was feasting for many days.

Koku and Kemi lived in Adia's house. Adia did not allow them to build a house of their own because she still wanted to look after Koku. She still thought of him as a child. Koku too did not want to live away from his mother.

They were happy together. Kemi's mother came often to see both Kemi and Koku. She too was happy. She was not poor any more now. She did not wear rags and she ate good food.

About a year after Koku and Kemi were married, their first baby arrived. It was a girl and everybody was very pleased. Adia was the happiest of them all.

She called the baby Kike. Koku was happy with the baby and Kemi loved it. What a lucky child! She had everything!

Adia was now very old. She did not go out much because she was not strong enough.

One night when she slept, she dreamt. The Lady-in-white came. Her white dress had a black line round it.

She did not look as happy as before and she spoke softly. "Tell Koku all about himself tomorrow morning,"she told Adia. "Tell him about the woman at Idiala.

This is the last time you will see me. You have been a good woman, go in peace. Good-bye."

As soon as she said this she turned and walked away. She did not look back. Adia did not want her to go.

"Stop!" Adia shouted, "Don't go yet. I still want to see you. Where am I going and who are you?"

The Lady-in-white did not answer.

In the morning Adia called Koku and Kemi into her room.

"Koku, I am going to tell you something. I fear that you may not still love me when you know. But I must tell you even though it makes me sad.

"I, Adia, am not your real mother. I found you by the stream near Idiala. You were born a twin child but in Idiala twins are not allowed to live. That woman in Idiala, the mother of Sanu, is your real mother. I wanted a child and my prayer was answered; I found you."

"That is enough, Mami," cried Koku, "I don't want any other mother than you. You have been my mother and you will always be my mother. If you had not found me, I would not have lived."

Koku was all the time kneeling by the bed where Adia lay. He held her hands and both of them wept. Kemi wept too. They were not sad, yet they wept.

"I am now very happy," said Adia, "I know you love me as you should love a mother. I shall give you all I have when I die."

The following day Adia died. Koku wept all day.

He and Kemi were very sad. So too were the women and children of Ihama.

Adia's funeral was like that of a queen. Everyone came to the funeral; men, women, young and old.

People came from all the towns and villages around.

Many came from Idiala. Adia had been like an angel among them. There was no other woman like her.

The people were happy that Koku, to whom she left all she had, was also good. His young wife was kind too. She called all the children together in one place and feasted them well,

Soon after this Koku paid a visit to Idiala. He went to Akila. "Call your wife," he asked Akila. "I want to talk to you both." When the three of them were seated, Koku said, "You perhaps wonder why I look like your wife, Abi, and her son, Sanu. I now know, I am her son and your son too. I am one of the twin children you threw away."

He told the story which Adia had told him. Abi jumped up, held him close and wept. Akila himself was happy. He drank more palm wine that day than usual.

Before long the news had passed round the village. The people came to Akila's house. They heard the story again and they were pleased that Koku was one of their people.

But many women wept because their twin children had been killed. They knew now that twin children were not evil. Perhaps their children had been brave, strong and handsome children like Koku. From that day twin children were welcome in the village. Their parents received many gifts and no one feared having twins any more. The bad old custom had died. Adia had killed it.

If Koku had not lived, thousands of twin children might have been killed since that day.